WELL I NEVER!

Text by
Heather Eyles

Pictures by
Tony Ross

The Overlook Press
Woodstock, New York

First published in 1990 by
The Overlook Press
Lewis Hollow Road
Woodstock, New York 12498

Library of Congress Cataloging-in-Publication Data

Eyles, Heather.
Well I never!

Summary: Polly tells her mother that she cannot get dressed for school
because a multitude of monsters, vampires, and other scary creatures are
trying on her clothes.
[1. Monsters—Fiction.   2. Clothing and dress—Fiction.
[I. Ross, Tony, ill.   II. Title.
PZ7.E974We   1989   [E]   89-16254
ISBN 0-87951-383-7

Printed in Italy by Grafiche AZ, Verona

It was Monday morning. Time to go to
school, and Polly wasn't dressed. As usual.

"Go and get your T-shirt," said Mom.
"It's in the bedroom."

"I can't go in there," said Polly. "There's
a witch in there."
"Nonsense!" said Mom.

"And your shorts are in the bathroom," said Mom.

"Oh, I can't go in there," said Polly.
"There's a vampire in there."
"Rubbish!" said Mom.

"By the way," said Mom, "your socks are on the stairs."

"Nope, I can't go up there," said Polly.
"There's a werewolf up there."
"Fiddlesticks!" said Mom.

"Don't forget, your shoes are in the cupboard under the stairs," said Mom.

"No, I'm not going in there," said Polly.
"There's a ghost in there."
"Balderdash!" said Mom.

So Mom went to get the clothes herself.
"Toads and slugs' bottoms!" shrieked the witch, who looked very fetching in Polly's T-shirt.

"What a lovely neck
you have, my dear!"
murmured the vampire,
who was just trying on
Polly's shorts.

"Grrr!" growled the
werewolf, who was
having a lovely slobbery
chew of Polly's socks.

The ghost said nothing.
Not anything at all. But
she did a spooky dance in
Polly's shoes.

Mom ran all the way back to the kitchen.
"Well I never!" she said.

"You're joking, aren't you, Mom?" asked
Polly.
"Am I?" asked Mom.
"There aren't really any monsters out
there, are there?" asked Polly.
"Aren't there?" asked Mom.

So they went out to look together, hand in hand, down the hall,

up the stairs,

past the bathroom,

and into the bedroom.

"Phew!" said Mom.

"Told you!" said Polly. "And now I think
I'll get dressed if you don't mind."